Dear Parents,

Welcome to the Scholastic Reader series. We have taken over 80 years of experience with teachers, parents, and children and put it into a program that is designed to match your child's interests and skills.

Level 1—Short sentences and stories made up of words kids can sound out using their phonics skills and words that are important to remember.

Level 2—Longer sentences and stories with words kids need to know and new "big" words that they will want to know.

Level 3—From sentences to paragraphs to longer stories, these books have large "chunks" of texts and are made up of a rich vocabulary.

Level 4—First chapter books with more words and fewer pictures.

It is important that children learn to read well enough to succeed in school and beyond. Here are ideas for reading this book with your child:

- Look at the book together. Encourage your child to read the title and make a prediction about the story.
- Read the book together. Encourage your child to sound out words when appropriate. When your child struggles, you can help by providing the word.
- Encourage your child to retell the story. This is a great way to check for comprehension.
- Have your child take the fluency test on the last page to check progress.

Scholastic Readers are designed to support your child's efforts to learn how to read at every age and every stage. Enjoy helping your child learn to read and love to read.

—Francie Alexander
Chief Education Officer
Scholastic Education

Library of Congress Cataloging-in-Publication Data.

Peterson, Scott.
Batman : the story of Batman / written by Scott Peterson ; illustrated by Rick Burchett.
p. cm. -- (Scholastic reader. Level 3)
"Batman created by Bob Kane."
"Cartwheel books."
Summary: Wealthy Bruce Wayne acquires the skills necessary to protect the people of Gotham City, adopting the disguise of a bat to safeguard his identity .
ISBN 0-439-47104-4 (pbk.)
[1. Heroes--Fiction. 2. Adventure and adventurers--Fiction.]
I. Burchett, Rick, ill. II. Title. III. Title: Batman. IV. Series.
PZ7.P445335Bak 2006

[E]--dc22   2005021271

10 9 8 7 6 5 4 3 2   06 07 08 09 10
Printed in the U.S.A. 23 • First printing, March 2006

THE STORY OF BATMAN

Written by **Scott Peterson**

Illustrated by **Rick Burchett**

Batman created by Bob Kane

Scholastic Reader — Level 3

SCHOLASTIC INC.

New York Toronto London Auckland Sydney
Mexico City New Delhi Hong Kong Buenos Aires

CHAPTER ONE

ONE AWFUL NIGHT

Bruce Wayne was one of the richest men in Gotham City. He lived in Wayne Manor, above a secret cave — the Batcave!

That's because Bruce was also Batman!

Every evening, Batman carefully checked his crime-fighting tools and equipment. Then he would go out on patrol.

THE WAYNE FAMILY
AT WAYNE MANOR.

Once, Bruce had been the luckiest little boy
in Gotham City. He had two loving parents, a
wonderful home, and even a butler.

But then one night, Bruce's parents were
killed. Young Master Bruce felt sad and lonely.
And now he knew that there were bad people
in the world.

He wanted to keep these bad people from hurting other people, but he didn't know how.

So Bruce decided to read how others have done it.

He took out books from the library on science, detective work, karate, and other martial arts. He taught himself boxing. But he still felt that he needed to learn more.

BRUCE STUDIES HARD.

WEIGHT TRAIN
Martial Arts
CHEMISTRY
PHYSICS
Fo
CRIME
DETECTION

He wanted to meet people who could teach him to use the things he had been reading about and practicing. So he decided to leave his home and find them.

Bruce said good-bye to Alfred Pennyworth, the Wayne family's butler. Alfred had raised Bruce since his parents died and was his closest friend. Bruce would miss him.

CHAPTER TWO

THE JOURNEY

Bruce set off for Alabama. A man was there who could help him.

This man was a detective. He taught Bruce how to track people. He taught Bruce how to talk to suspects and how to trust his instincts. Bruce had never been able to learn these things from books.

Next Bruce left the country and went to Asia. There he studied with a martial arts master named Master Kirigi.

First, Master Kirigi ignored Bruce for a month. He didn't think Bruce really wanted to learn martial arts. Then he realized Bruce wasn't going to leave. So Master Kirigi showed Bruce the right way to sweep a floor. A month later, he taught Bruce the proper way to cook rice. All the time, Bruce was learning patience.

Finally, Master Kirigi taught Bruce about secret martial arts and healing. He taught Bruce how to kick and defend himself in any situation.

Bruce learned quickly and became very good. But he wanted to continue his travels.

So he thanked Master Kirigi and left.

BRUCE LEARNED QUICKLY.

In Paris, Bruce met a man named Henri Ducard. Henri taught Bruce how to find anyone. Bruce learned how to hear quiet conversations, how to blend into shadows and disappear.

Henri asked Bruce to stay on as his assistant. But Bruce had other plans. So he thanked Henri and left.

BRUCE LEARNED TO BLEND INTO THE SHADOWS.

Everywhere Bruce went, he met someone who taught him something new.

One man taught Bruce how to escape from any trap.

Another man taught Bruce how to disguise himself so even Alfred wouldn't recognize him.

In Italy, Bruce learned how to drive like a professional race car driver.

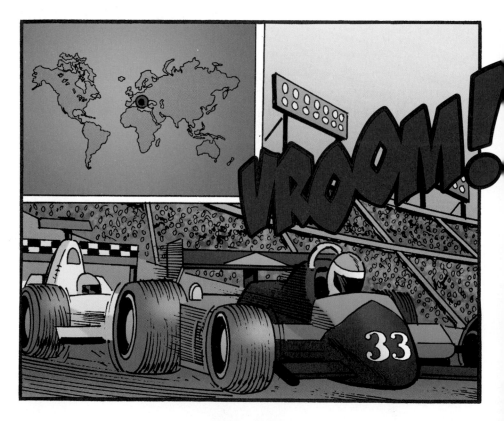

In Russia, Bruce learned how to fly any kind of plane or helicopter.

In China, Bruce learned how to stay awake with only fifteen minutes of sleep a night.

Bruce knew he was getting closer to his goal. He had the skills he needed to fight crime.

But would they be enough?

CHAPTER THREE

THE FIRST STEP

Back in Gotham at last, Bruce felt it was time to use his skills.

He decided to wear a ski mask. No one could know Bruce Wayne, famous Gotham billionaire, was walking around the most dangerous parts of the city.

BRUCE WORE A DISGUISE SO HE WOULD NOT BE RECOGNIZED.

As he walked along the streets, Bruce kept his eyes open. He needed to be alert for any signs of trouble.

Just then, he saw two men. They were loading motorcycles into a truck outside a store. The store's window had been smashed. Bruce was sure the men had stolen them.

"Stop!" Bruce said as he stepped in front of the men. "You must put those bikes back."

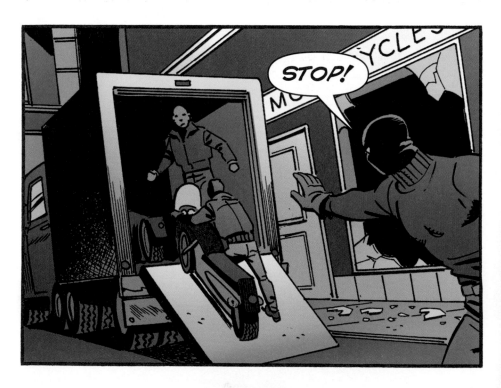

The men looked at each other. They laughed.

"Who are you?" one man asked.

"And what are you going to do about it?" said the other man. Then they loaded the last motorcycle, shut the door, and drove off.

Bruce shook his head. Nothing had gone as he had thought. He didn't help anyone. He didn't stop crime. His plan hadn't worked.

CHAPTER FOUR

THE BAT

Bruce sat in the dark library of Wayne Manor. He'd thought if he worked hard, he could go out and fight crime. But it wasn't that easy.

Bruce looked up at the picture of his parents over the fireplace.

"Mother, Father, please help me," he said. "I don't know what to do. I want to help people, but I don't know how. I've trained and I've studied, but it's not enough. There's something I'm missing, but I don't know what it is."

CRASH! A window shattered. A bat flew into the room.

Bruce stared at the bat. It was the biggest one he'd ever seen. It perched on the mantel over the fireplace and stared back at him.

Bruce shivered. He had always been afraid of bats. When he was a little boy, he fell into an enormous bat cave underneath the backyard. He was there for an hour waiting for his father to rescue him.

A bat. That was the answer. Bats were scary. He would scare the bad people. He would become a bat!

Bruce began working on his costume. He used materials made by his company, Wayne Enterprises. Bruce found a special suit that resisted fire and a cape that spread around him like wings.

BATARANG

BAT-GRENADE

BATCUFFS

FLAME-RESISTANT CAPE

Bruce created all kinds of weapons, including the Batarang, the Bat-grenade, and Batcuffs. They all fit on a special Utility Belt.

Bruce then discovered a unique car, built by Wayne Enterprises, that could go very fast. He could drive the car using voice commands, and it had built-in computers.

In a few months, Bruce was ready to test out his new identity.

CHAPTER FIVE

A NEW BEGINNING

Late one night, some men were stealing television sets from a store. They worked quickly and quietly.

Suddenly, a dark shape leaped right in front of them! *WHOOSH!*

The men were terrified!

Three of them simply froze, not moving a muscle. Another dropped to his knees. The last man tried to run away.

There was a slight rustling sound and a dark blur. A large shape swooped to the ground.

THE CRIMINALS WERE TERRIFIED!

None of the men knew exactly what had happened. They only knew that this thing had moved faster than they could see and then disappeared. But from the darkness came a terrifying, whispering voice.

"Tell your friends," the voice said. "Tell all your friends. Gotham is protected by Batman!"

CHAPTER SIX

THE PENGUIN

GOTHAM BECAME SAFER BECAUSE OF BATMAN.

GOTHAM GAZETTE

GOTHAM SAFE!

BATMAN BRINGS BACK THE NIGHT

Bruce had been disguised as Batman for three months. And already he could see how much better Gotham had become.

The streets were safer at night. And news of the giant crime-fighting bat had spread quickly.

Now just the sight of Batman was often enough to stop crimes from happening.

Then one night, Batman noticed four men standing around a fire in an alley. When he saw them looking around nervously, Batman became suspicious.

One man took a very large diamond out of his coat and handed it to one of the others. Batman decided to make his move.

ONE MAN TOOK A DIAMOND FROM HIS POCKET.

He dropped down into the alley, sticking close to the shadows.

"Good evening, gentlemen," Batman said.

The men jumped.

"Batman," one man whispered.

Quickly, they hid the diamond. Then three of the men took off running.

Staying in the shadows, Batman ran after the men. They didn't hear Batman behind them. Batman caught up quickly.

He slammed the heads of the two largest men together. *CRACK!*

As the third man turned around, Batman dropped to the ground. He stuck his leg out, sweeping it forward.

The man found his own legs were suddenly out in front of him—instead of holding him up. *BAM!* He fell on his back, hard.

Then the fourth man walked up to
Batman. The man smiled.

"And a good evening to you, too, Batman,"
the man said.

Batman looked at this odd person. He was
quite short and wasn't dressed anything like
the others. He wore fancy clothes and a top
hat, and he carried a cane.

Then Batman recognized the man from the newspapers. It was Oswald Cobblepot, a criminal genius. But he was known by another name.

"You are the Penguin, I believe," Batman said.

The Penguin laughed. "Ah, I see we've heard of each other."

The Penguin looked down at the men lying on the ground. "The stories about you seem to be quite true, Batman," the Penguin said.

"So are the stories about you," Batman said. "You have the Genleigh diamond that was stolen last night." Batman took the huge diamond from the Penguin's hand.

The Penguin nodded. "Indeed I do. I was trying to get it back for its owner when you arrived."

BATMAN TOOK THE DIAMOND FROM THE PENGUIN'S HAND.

"You're saying you weren't behind the theft?" Batman asked.

"Oh, no, no," said the Penguin, shaking his head. He smiled. "And you can't prove otherwise."

Meanwhile, the police had arrived and led the thieves away.

As the Penguin stepped into a long black limousine, he said, "I'm sure we'll see each other again, Batman!"

Batman realized that cleaning up Gotham might be harder than he had thought. Some criminals used their brains more than their fists.

Batman smiled. No matter how difficult it was, he had a job to do. And at last he knew he could do it!

Fluency Fun

The words in each list below end in the same sounds.
Read the words in a list.
Read them again.
Read them faster.
Try to read all 15 words in one minute.

carefully	**curious**	**created**
finally	**dangerous**	**decided**
lonely	**enormous**	**protected**
quietly	**nervous**	**resisted**
suddenly	**suspicious**	**trusted**

Look for these words in the story.

unique	**genius**	**equipment**
special	**patience**	

Note to Parents:

According to *A Dictionary of Reading and Related Terms*, fluency is "the ability to read smoothly, easily, and readily with freedom from word-recognition problems." Fluency is necessary for good comprehension and enjoyable reading. The activities on this page include a speed drill and a sight-recognition drill. Speed drills build fluency because they help students rapidly recognize common syllables and spelling patterns in words, and they're fun! Sight-recognition drills help students smoothly and accurately recognize words. Practice these activities with your child to help him or her become a fluent reader.

—Wiley Blevins
Reading Specialist